What's Inside Me?
My Heart and Blood

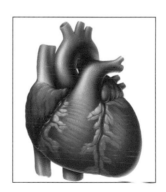

Dana Meachen Rau

BENCHMARK BOOKS

MARSHALL CAVENDISH
NEW YORK

My Heart
and Blood

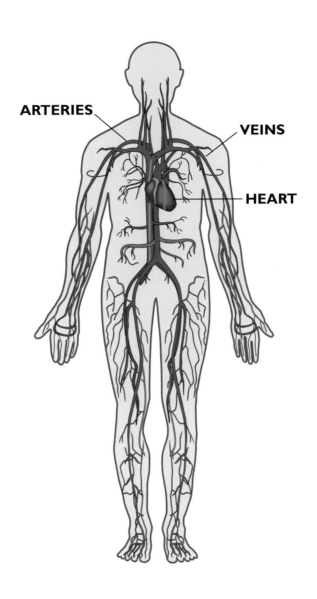

ARTERIES

VEINS

HEART

Put your hand on your chest. You might be able to feel your heart beating. Your heart is always working. It pumps blood around your body.

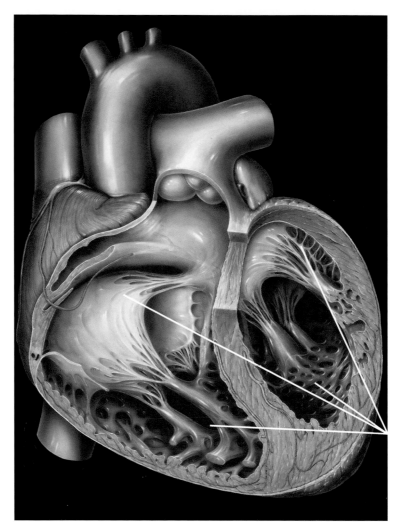

CHAMBERS

Your heart is shaped like a bumpy ball. The rib bones in your chest protect it.

This bumpy ball is hollow inside. It is divided into four parts called *chambers*.

Blood goes into your heart and out again.

The blood travels all over your body. Your heart sends it to your head, your arms and legs, and all your inside parts, too. Then the blood travels back to the heart.

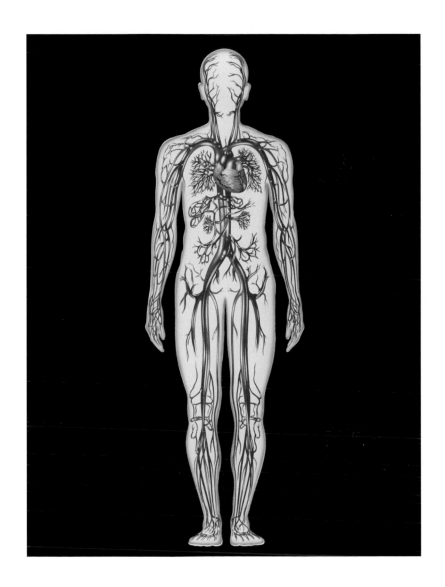

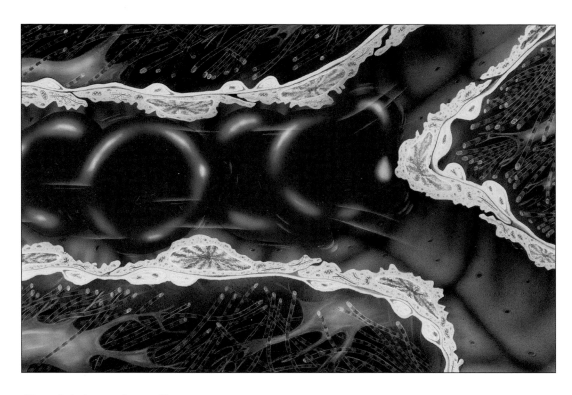

Red blood cells

Your body needs blood because blood is filled with *oxygen*.

Oxygen helps your arms and legs move. It helps you think and breathe.

Red blood cells carry oxygen to all parts of your body.

Blood carries *nutrients* from the food you eat. Your body needs these nutrients to grow.

Blood also collects waste from parts of your body. Waste is material your body cannot use.

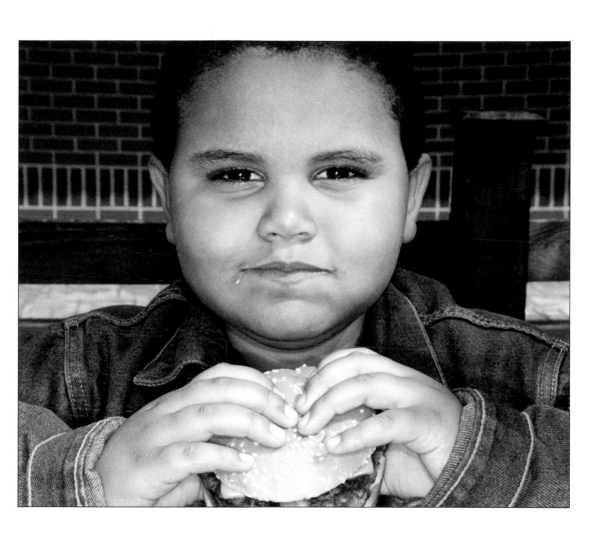

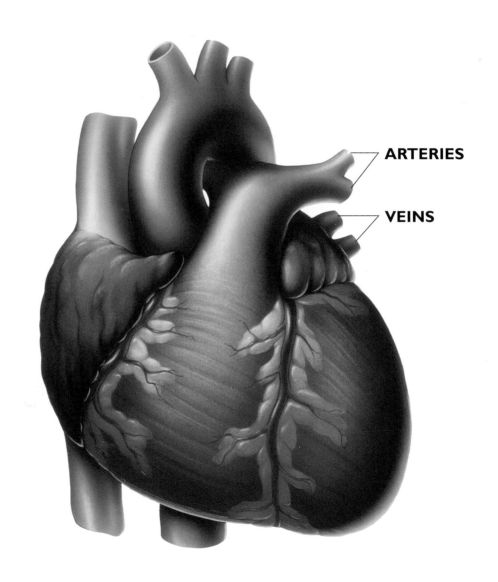

ARTERIES

VEINS

14

Your heart pumps blood to the body through *arteries*. Arteries are tubes that carry blood away from your heart.

Blood goes back to your heart through tubes called *veins*.

Some arteries and veins are so small that you cannot see them. They are called *capillaries*.

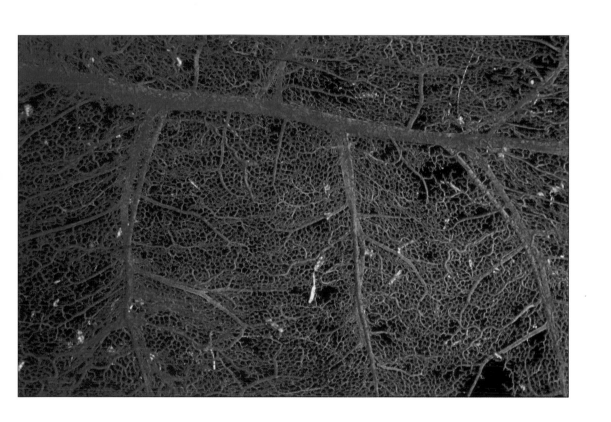

When you exercise, your heart pumps fast. That is because your body needs a lot of oxygen and nutrients to work hard.

When you sleep, your body is resting. Your heart pumps slowly.

The *white blood cells* in
your blood are in charge
of protecting your body.
They fight *germs*.

Have you ever cut your finger?
You may have seen a drop
of blood. Germs can get into
that cut.

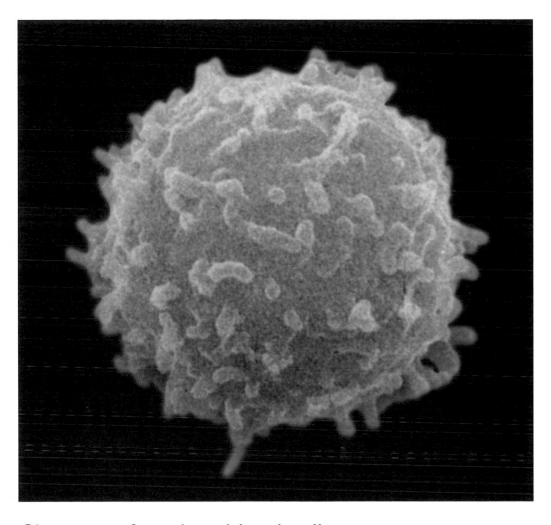

Close-up of a white blood cell

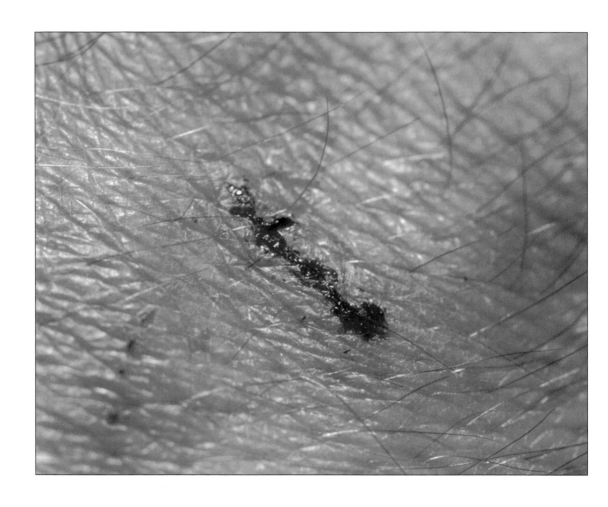

Around your cut, blood gets thicker and thicker. Then it clots, or closes, making a scab. Germs cannot get in.

Your body keeps your blood clean. Blood passes through the kidneys. The kidneys clean the blood.

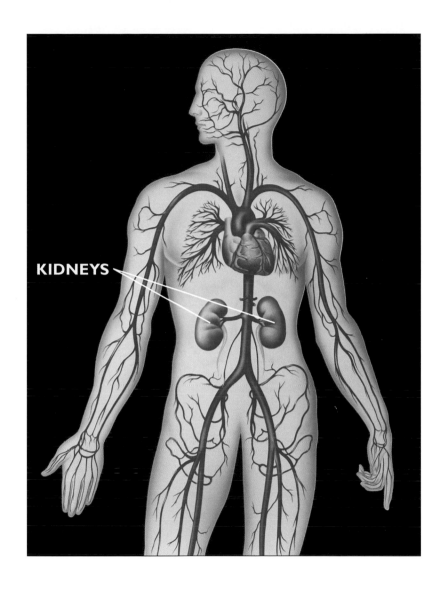

KIDNEYS

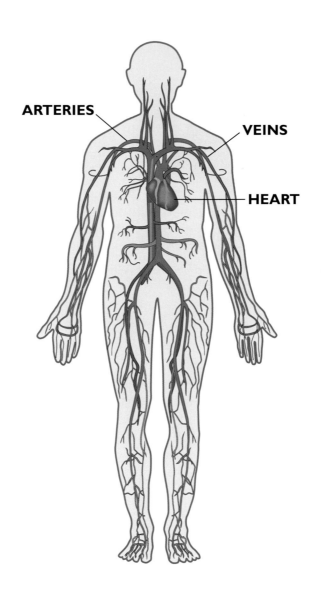

ARTERIES

VEINS

HEART

Your heart, blood, arteries, and veins are called your *circulatory system*.

Sometimes your heart pumps fast. Sometimes it pumps slow. But it is always pumping and keeping you alive.

Challenge Words

arteries (AR-tuh-rees)—Tubes that carry blood to all parts of your body.

capillaries (KAP-uh-ler-ees)—Very small arteries and veins.

chambers—The open spaces inside your heart.

circulatory system (SUR-kyuh-luh-tor-ee SIS-tuhm)—Your heart, blood, arteries, and veins.

germs—Something that can make you sick.

nutrients (NEW-tree-uhnts)—The parts of food your body needs to stay healthy.

oxygen (OK-si-juhn)—The part of air your body needs to work.

red blood cells—The part of the blood that carries oxygen.

veins—Tubes that carry blood to your heart.

white blood cells—The part of the blood that fights germs.

Index

Page numbers in **boldface** are illustrations.

With thanks to Nanci Vargus, Ed.D. and Beth Walker Gambro, reading consultants

Benchmark Books
Marshall Cavendish
99 White Plains Road
Tarrytown, New York 10591-9001
www.marshallcavendish.com

Library of Congress Cataloging-in-Publication Data

Rau, Dana Meachen, 1971–
My heart and blood / by Dana Meachen Rau.
p. cm. — (Bookworms: What's inside me?)
Includes index.
ISBN 0-7614-1779-6
1. Cardiovascular system—Juvenile literature. I. Title. II. Series.

QP103.R38 2004
612.1—dc22
2004002512

Photo Research by Anne Burns Images

Cover photo by *Jay Mallin*

The photographs in this book are used with the permission and through the courtesy of:
Photo Researchers: pp. 1, 14 Brian Evans; p. 6 Medical Art Service; pp. 9, 25 John Bavosi; p. 10 Michel Gilles;
p. 17 Biophoto Association. *Jay Mallin*: p. 2. *Corbis*: p. 5 Royalty Free; p. 13 Pat Doyle; p. 18 Richard Gross;
p. 29 Jim Cummins. *Visuals Unlimited*: p. 21 Dr. Donald Fawcett & E. Shelton. *Custom Medical Stock Photo*: p. 22.

Series design by Becky Terhune

Printed in China
1 3 5 6 4 2